Meet the Characterz

Melvin Meadly

Dan

DI Meadly

Priti Kaur

Death's head hawkmoth

Worker 33137

Mr Johnson

Mrs Whelks

Norman Crudwell

For Mum, who used to keep bees
and now just admires them

OXFORD
UNIVERSITY PRESS

Great Clarendon Street, Oxford OX2 6DP

Oxford University Press is a department of the University of Oxford.
It furthers the University's objective of excellence in research, scholarship, and
education by publishing worldwide. Oxford is a registered trade mark of Oxford
University Press in the UK and in certain other countries

British Library Cataloguing in Publication Data

Data available

ISBN: 978-0-19-276387-7

1 3 5 7 9 10 8 6 4 2

Printed in China

Paper used in the production of this book is a natural,
recyclable product made from wood grown in sustainable forests.
The manufacturing process conforms to the environmental
regulations of the country of origin.

BEE BOY

Clash of the Killer Queens

Tony De Saulles

OXFORD
UNIVERSITY PRESS

From my bedroom window I can see green fields far away on the edge of town. Dan said there used to be a meadow right here but they ploughed it up to build our block of flats. There are fifty families living in Meadow Tower and we live at the top.

Dan used to live in the flat next door.
At first he was just our next-door
neighbour but then he became our friend.
He didn't really have a job but he knew
a lot. His best subjects were nature and
saving planet Earth.

'We're lucky to be living here,
Mel,' he'd say.

Most planets in the universe are too hot, too cold or poisonous but we live somewhere with all the ingredients for life. It's a planet in a billion and we need to look after it!

Dan doesn't live in Meadow Tower any more. I miss him.

Mum calls out from the kitchen,

Breakfast!

For breakfast I have honey on my toast but for tea I like cheese or scrambled eggs. We eat quick food because Mum's always tired when she gets back from the police station.

Detective Inspector Meadly, that's my mum. Seeing so much bad stuff makes her worry.

I spotted some of your mates messing around in the shopping centre at lunchtime.

I don't have any mates and, anyway, the people she saw would have been older than me. I munch my toast and honey and think about bees.

My bees.

Today is a VERY important day. There are 50,000 bees in our beehive and after school I'm going to open it up and look inside. I need to check that they're making new bees to keep the hive alive and making honey too. I've done it lots of times before but never on my own.

It was a few months ago when Dan found the hive at the dump and brought it home. It needed mending but Dan was good at that sort of thing. He did a sketch to show me how beehives work. It's on my pinboard.

X-RAY VIEW INSIDE BEEHIVE

levels 1 and 2 = honeycomb cells full of honey

lid

front door

ledge

level 3 = honeycomb cells full of baby bees (eggs hatch into larvae – larvae hatch into bees and bees = honey!)

'You're going to be a bee-keeper!' he said.
'It's important work but it will be fun.'

And it was fun. Brilliant fun. I was
hooked immediately and I've been bee-crazy
ever since.

'We'll give the bees a home and they'll give
us honey!' Dan said.

'Like rent?'

'Yeah, sort of.' He laughed.

We bought some bees from Dan's mum,
Daisy. Daisy lives near Meadow Tower and
keeps beehives at the bottom of her garden.

'Bees love living in towns,' she told us.
'Away from farmland that is sprayed with
harmful chemicals.'

So guess where we put ours?

7

We've got the highest beehive in England, Mel! Our bees can see every park and garden for miles around. How cool is that?

Our bees love their high hive and are always busy buzzing around the town gardens collecting pollen and nectar and bringing it back to the roof. When Dan was here he'd wait until I got back from school and we'd check on the bees together. He'd chat and joke with Mr Johnson, who grows flowers and vegetables in pots. Mr Johnson is interested in bees and keeps an eye on things when I'm not there.

The bee-keeping went well when Dan and I first started but then, disaster – our bees were attacked. It was like a battle scene. Bee wings, legs and heads were scattered all around. Dan said the attackers had eaten some of our baby bees and honey too.

'Who did this?' I asked.

'Probably wasps,' Dan said. 'A deadly killer. Honeybees have lots of enemies including microscopic mites and death's head hawkmoths.'

I'm eating supermarket honey on my toast this morning but that's going to change. Dan left the hive and the bee equipment and today is the day when I take charge. If my bees are happy and healthy I'll be eating Meadow Tower honey in a few weeks.

Mum squeezes my shoulder.

'Eat your toast and go to school!'

I keep my head down when I walk to school.

'Don't draw attention to yourself and people won't bother you,' Mum says.

The kids at school don't get it. I've tried to explain that bee-keeping is cool but nobody's interested. Maybe they'll listen next week when it's my turn to read my project at assembly. It's called BEES ARE BRILLIANT and I'm going to have a practice in the library at lunchtime. Mrs Gashkori, the librarian, is going to listen and offer advice. Mrs Gashkori says the whole school will be bee-crazy after my talk.

I'm walking up the school steps.

'Melvin Meadly! Here, please.'

It's Mrs Whelks, my teacher.

'Ben Flemming is ill,' she says.

'Yes, Miss?' I reply.

I'VE GOT TO READ MY PROJECT TODAY?

'But I'm not... I haven't practised...'

'Nonsense! What's it about? Bugs or something?' Mrs Whelks asks. Then without waiting for an answer she heads for the staffroom. 'You'll be fine. Come up on stage after register,' she shouts.

But maybe this is my chance. My project is written and I've even got my bee-keeper's suit in my backpack (I was going to show it to Mrs Gashkori at lunchtime). I think I'm ready.

The registers have been called. This is it. The whole school is waiting with excitement to hear my project.

But I'm trembling as I step on to the school stage.

My bee-keeper's suit has a hood with mesh at the front to keep bees out. I can normally see OK but the hall lights are very bright so I'm walking like a nervous zombie.

Three hundred confused faces stare up at me.

'And now Melvin Meadly is going to give his talk about...'

Mrs Whelks peers down at her notes.

'Bees! Quickly, Melvin, step forward.'

Nobody claps as I make my way to the front of the stage.

I clear my throat.

17

Good morning. Some of you may already know that I am a bee-keeper and today I am going to tell you all about my bees...

...For human beings to stay alive we need plants to eat. But plants need bees to pollinate them so they can reproduce and make more plants. That is why bees are SO important. NO BEES, NO WORLD!

Phew! It's going OK. They seem interested – even the new girl in our class, Priti Kaur. Excellent.

But honeybees are in trouble...

Eh? There's something buzzing in my hood!

BZZZ!

...when farmers spray their crops with chemicals...

Bzzz!

...A BEE!

There's sniggering from the audience as I struggle to unzip my hood. I know I shouldn't panic but I can't help it.

HOW DID IT GET IN? IT'S GOING TO STING ME ON THE FACE!

BZZZ!

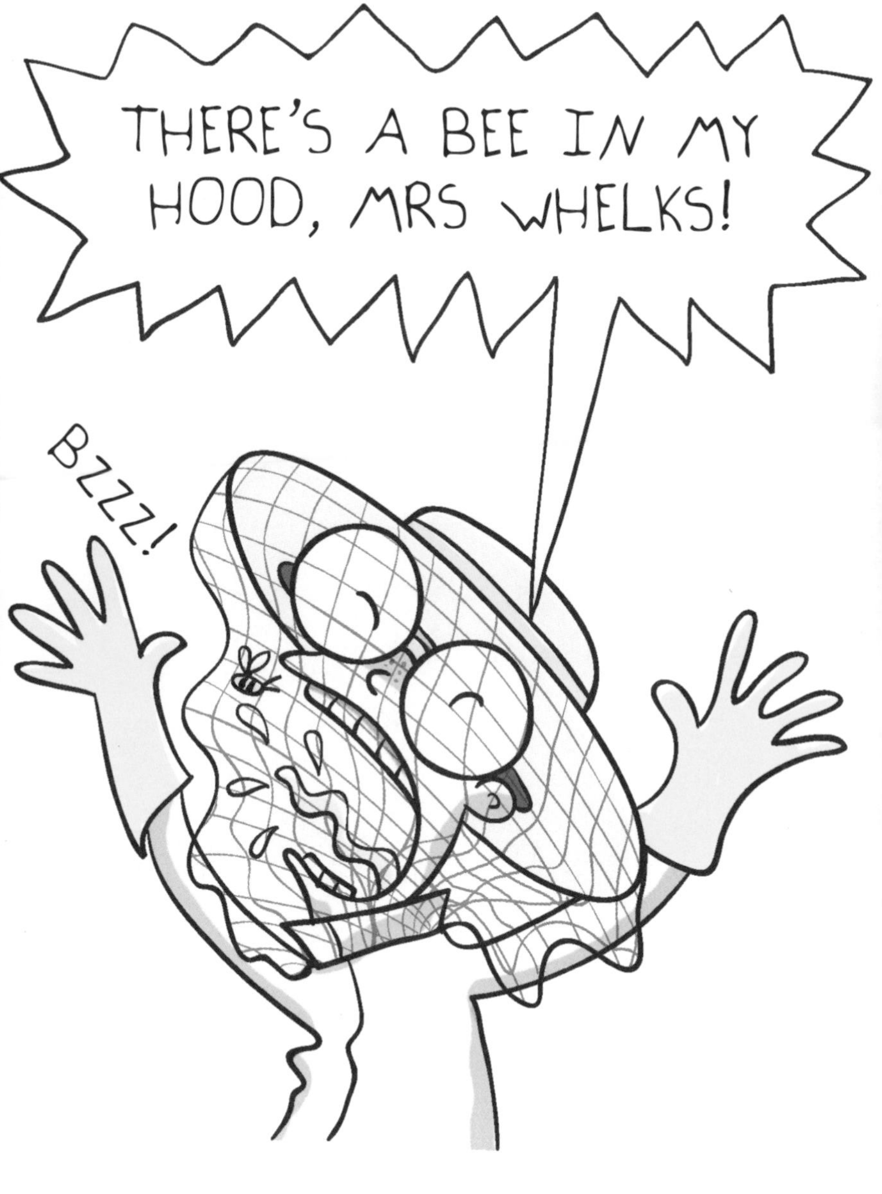
THERE'S A BEE IN MY HOOD, MRS WHELKS!
BZZZ!

The chuckles turn to laughter. Somebody at the front starts buzzing.

It's troublemaker, Norman Crudwell.

BZZZZZZZZ!

Mrs Whelks tuts and fumbles impatiently for the zip on my hood.

KEEP STILL!

Mrs Whelks is retiring soon. (Hooray!) I hope our new teacher isn't as grumpy as Mrs Whelks.

Now the rest of the school has joined in.

BZZZZZZZZZZZZ!

'The bee suit was a silly idea, Melvin,'
Mrs Whelks hisses under her breath when
she finally finds the zip.

'You should have...

EEEK!'

BZZZ!

23

The bee whizzes out, does two loop-the-loops and disappears up Mrs Whelks's dress.

She's dancing around the stage – singing too!

25

The three hundred faces are now staring at Mrs Whelks's pants.

VZZIP!

She has been stung on the bottom.

OWWWCH!

Crudwell snorts
with joy.

Nice one,
Bee Boy!

BEE BOY?
Where did that
come from?

Seconds later,
everybody's
chanting...

Beetroot-faced Mrs Whelks has had enough...

SILENCE! NORMAN AND MELVIN, SEE ME AFTER MORNING BREAK – YOU CAN CLEAN OUT STINKY AND WHIFFER, THE SCHOOL GERBILS. NOW BACK TO THE CLASSROOM!

Brilliant. Now Mrs Whelks has got it in for me and Crudwell is being punished too. They're going to make my life hell.

And what about 'Bee Boy', my new nickname? I guess it doesn't sound too bad but I don't think they meant it as a compliment.

The school day seems to take FOREVER but 3:30 finally arrives and I scurry home. At Meadow Tower the lift is out of order again. I don't mind using the stairs except I have to go past Crudwell's door and he is the last person I want to see. I should be OK because he's usually indoors playing computer games (if there's a game that involves blowing things up, Crudwell's got it).

I hear a voice.

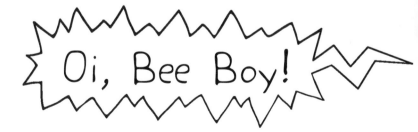

Oi, Bee Boy!

Blast, I've been spotted and there's that nickname again.

'Off to get some of your horrible honey?' Crudwell sneers.

What does he mean HORRIBLE? I try to explain, 'Honey is one of nature's miracles... delicious natural sweetness!'

Eating gunge from insects' bottoms IS *NOT* natural, you nerdy numpty! Stick with chips – that's what Mum says. Chips and ice cream – chips *IN* ice cream! That's REAL food!

I give up. It doesn't matter what I say, Crudwell will have an answer – he always does.

'And keep your stingy little bugs in your hive. When they come in our house we squish 'em with our slippers!'

'Don't kill them – just put them out the window!' I think. But I don't say it.

I set off up the next lot of stairs.

'See you later, Bee Boy!' Crudwell shouts.

33

I shut the front door behind me and lean against it with a sigh. It's so great to be home.

Mum appears from the living room. 'Good day, love?' she asks.

Might as well get it over with.

'Ben Flemming was ill so I gave my talk a week early.'

'Really? How'd it go?'

'Not too bad,' I say. Well, no point in both of us being miserable.

'Did you wear your bee-keeper's suit?'

'Yep – it was a great idea,' I lie. But I don't want to discuss it any more so I escape to my bedroom.

When I open the window for some fresh air two bees fly in. They circle above my head then disappear back outside. Odd!

I pull on my bee-keeper's suit and gather other equipment that I'll need. My heart is thumping but I don't want Mum to know that opening the hive is such a big deal. If she sees I'm nervous she'll start stressing and that's when Mum stops me doing stuff.

'Just popping out!' I call and quickly disappear. A minute later I've climbed the stairs and opened the door that leads out on to the roof.

Empty cola cans and crisp packets have been dumped on the hive roof but the bees don't seem to mind.

'I see Norman and his mates have been making a mess again!'

It's Mr Johnson. He brings a bin bag over and holds it open while I clear the litter away.

'Checking the bees on your own?' he asks. 'No Dan?'

'Dan's gone,' I say. 'I'm looking after the bees now.'

Mr Johnson is surprised. 'Gone? He never said anything to me.'

He didn't say much to me either, I think. But I don't want to have to explain to Mr Johnson how much I miss Dan. And I think Mum misses him too. He said he'd email us but we haven't heard from him yet.

Mr Johnson nods like he understands my silence. 'Need a hand?' he asks.

I feel like I should really be able to do this on my own but I'm relieved at the offer of help.

'Thanks, Mr Johnson. Dan left his bee-keeper's suit; I'll run back and get it.'

Five minutes later, Mr Johnson has squeezed into Dan's suit and is ready to help.

'We need to light the smoker,' I say.

Bee-keepers all over the world do this. Smoke calms bees down and this makes it safer and easier to check inside a hive.

Mr Johnson holds the smoker steady as I light a bit of scrunched-up newspaper and drop it in. Next I add wood shavings that soon catch light and as I add more they start to smoke. I close the smoker and pump the bellows.

'You've got that smoking well!' Mr Johnson laughs as I lift the hive lid just a crack and puff smoke in. There's a gentle buzz from inside.

COUGH!

SPLUTTER!

SPLUTTER!

COUGH!

But the smoker is working TOO well and I'm soon wrapped in a blanket of smoke. I can hear Mr Johnson coughing but I can't see him.

The smoke spirals around me and lifts me off my feet! For just a moment, I'm hovering.

Then I'm falling, gently drifting down through the whiteness.

FLOOMF!

I land with a bump...

40

...somewhere warm and dark with gentle humming all around.

Buzzing bodies are bumping into me and poking me gently with investigating prods. The air is thick with a sweet, smoky smell. Wow! This is a lovely, calm place. But where am I?

As my eyes become accustomed to the dim light I find myself face to face with...

A BEE!

I am inside my own beehive? This is completely mad. And then I notice something even crazier when I look down and realize...

I AM A BEE!

One of the workers steps forward. She is small with tattered wings and a broken antenna but she has friendly smile.

'We'z all haz numberz, Marzter!' she says. 'I am worker 33137'.

'Er, hello,' I reply, in as normal a voice as I can manage.

'Come wiz uzzz!' 33137 says, setting off along a honeycomb path with open cells on either side. Other bees follow calling out as we go.

'Zum cells full of pollen!'
'Zum wizz honey!'
'And zum wizz babeez!'

I peer down into the open honeycomb cells. Tiny maggot-like larvae are hatching from eggs and wriggling about in liquid food. Nurse bees are tending to them.

Nurze beez work hard, Marzter!

We leave the path and enter an open area filling fast with a crowd of excited bees. In the centre, standing very still, is a huge bee. Like an aircraft in a hangar that is serviced by mechanics, she is being cleaned and fed by more nurse bees.

Woah! Is this Queen Bee?

Yezz, Marzter!

We feedz her royal jelly!

Growz bigger - live longer!

She lay thousandz of eggz to make new beez!

The queen approaches. Her wings vibrate gently and the nurse bees scamper away.

ZWEEEEE!

It's the call of the Queen Bee telling everybody that she is in charge.

'I'ze your Queen Bee and I'ze very pleazzzed to meet you, Marzter. Come! Sit wizz me and watch,' she says.

Once again the crowd pulls back to form a circle. A bee enters the space. It's 33137! She starts to dance, rotating and waggling her bottom in the air.

I think about Dan. If only he could see this – 'I'M INSIDE OUR HIVE AND WATCHING THE WAGGLE DANCE!'

But this dance is not for fun. It is a
message – a map telling the bees where a
rich patch of flowers can be found: what
direction they must travel from the sun
and how far away this treasure trove of
nectar and pollen is.

The dance continues, other bees join in
and I find myself dancing with them,
waggling and wiggling in excited circles.

'NO DANCE, NO FOOD!' Queen Bee cries. 'NO FOOD, NO HIVE!'

And a thousand buzzing insect voices reply in a deafening cry.

THE HIVE MUZST SURVIVE!

Pushing through the dancing bees, I join 33137 and together we waggle and turn in hypnotizing circles.

The Queen Bee speaks.

You hazz worked hard sisterz. We hazz lotz of honey and lotz of new beez. Weezar getting overcrowded. It izz almost time for some of uzz to swarm and leave!

The hive is excited to hear this news.

They continue to chant until 33137 collapses in an exhausted heap.

'Are you OK?' I ask, stepping forward to help...

PLOOFFF!

I'm back on the roof standing in a thinning cloud of smoke. Mr Johnson is still coughing and wiping his eyes.

'Perhaps a few less wood shavings next time, Melvin,' he splutters, waving the last of the smoke away. 'We're trying to calm the bees not kill them!'

Huh? Doesn't he want to know where I've been? He's acting like nothing's happened!

But what HAS happened? I'm not sure myself and I can't possibly explain it to Mr Johnson so I pretend nothing's happened too.

'Sorry, Mr Johnson, let's lift the lid and look inside.'

I don't really need to do this because I know exactly what's going on in there but I can't tell Mr Johnson.

The bees stay calm as we check the honeycomb frames. We can see clearly that the hive is doing well and Mr Johnson is impressed.

'I'm no bee expert, Melvin, but your hive's pretty full. I think they're almost ready to swarm!'

'Everything OK, love?' Mum asks as I munch my toast the next morning. 'You're looking very thoughtful staring at that jar of honey!'

'Huh? Yeah, I mean, no, nothing's wrong,' I mutter, continuing with my thoughts.

Did I REALLY turn into a bee, yesterday? Will it happen again? Can I go back? Are my bees going to swarm? Could I catch the swarm? I'd need another hive...but I'd have twice as much honey...

My thoughts are broken when Mum grabs the honey jar and clears the table.

'Time for school. I bet they'll all be chatting about you and your bees!' Mum says.

And she's not wrong.

◇◇◇◇◇◇◇◇

Yesterday's assembly hasn't been forgotten and just as I feared, it starts as soon as I get in the playground.

'Hey, Bee Boy, do you wear special pants like Mrs Whelks?' somebody shouts.

Crudwell joins in. 'Yeah, yellow and black striped bee pants?' he jeers. 'With a little hole for your stinger?'

I see Priti Kaur chuckling. I'm a joke and the whole school is laughing at me.

Even Mrs Whelks tuts and shakes her head when I come into class. I notice she's wearing a sort of home-made bee-proof outfit: trousers with bicycle clips. At least I'm guessing that's what it is because Mrs Whelks NEVER wears trousers and she doesn't ride a bike.

I hear quiet whisperings of, 'Bee Boy! Bee Boy!' from Crudwell and his mates but they soon shut up when Mrs Whelks looks up from the register and growls.

I keep to myself for the rest of the day. Walking home I spot Priti ahead. She turns into Meadow Tower. So she lives here too? I want to run after her – explain that bees are cool and I'm not a joke. But, of course, I don't.

The lift's still broken and, oh no, Crudwell's seen me.

'Following your new girlfriend, Bee Boy?' he sneers.

I splutter, 'What? I don't...

61

'I've seen how you look at her with your lovey-dovey eyes!'

I wish I was a bee again – a massive one. I'd jump on Crudwell and sting him – JAB, JAB, JAB!

'GET LOST, CRUDWELL!'

Did I just say that?

'Oooh, bit sensitive, are we?' He sniggers but looks surprised.

I carry on up the stairs but slow down when I see Priti.

She's laughing. SUCH A LOSER!

she calls out, not even bothering to look round.

And I hoped we might be friends.

I wait for Priti to get well ahead then plod slowly up to the flat, feeling sad and a little bit sick inside.

63

'Come on, glum face,' Mum says. 'Tell me what's up.'

But I can't. If I tell Mum about school she'll go into DI Meadly mode and talk to the head and that would be tragic. And entering the hive? That's GOT to stay a secret. I know Mum loves me and wants to help and all that but I need to sort this out on my own.

Armed with wood shavings, matches and smoker I climb the stairs to the roof, but there's even more misery when I get there. Somebody has sprayed graffiti on my beehive.

'BUZZ OFF, BEE BOY!' it says in big black letters.

Crudwell? I can't prove it. I wish Dan was here, he'd sort him out.

The paint has dried hard. I'll have to wait until my bees are snoozing in the winter before I can sand it down and repaint. I guess I've got more important stuff to do, anyway. I want to get back inside the hive. I want to be a bee again. I need to find out what's going on in there.

I look around to check that I'm alone — excellent, no Mr Johnson and no Crudwell. With shaking hands I light my smoker and it's soon puffing away. I stand, waiting for the smoke to spiral and then that gentle falling down, down, down to where my friends the bees are waiting.

But nothing.

I puff some more. Have I forgotten something? Is anything different this time? There's no Mr Johnson but surely that doesn't matter?

PUFF, PUFF, PUFF!

Nothing.

After half an hour I give up. I can't make it happen.

So, is that it?

I guess, for now, I'll have to check my bees like normal bee-keepers do. The smoke has done its work so I lift the lid and I'm pleased to see that the bees haven't swarmed.

But that's the only good thing that's happened today.

◯◯◯◯◯◯◯

I change my mind and talk to Mum. Not about everything, just the graffiti, but I must admit it helps to chat.

Cheese on toast with a bit of salad?

Typical Mum. She's always trying to cheer me up with food.

'Yes, please,' I say. 'But what am I going to do, Mum? They lean their bikes against the hive, cover it in litter and now this graffiti!'

'You mean what are WE going to do?'
she says. 'WE'RE going to politely ask
everybody in Meadow Tower to leave
your bees alone. We'll design a leaflet
and post it through every door...
TONIGHT!

After tea we get to work. Mum says
they're my bees and I should do the
writing but she'll help with the design
and printing.

By seven o'clock we're
posting our freshly
printed leaflets
through
letter boxes.

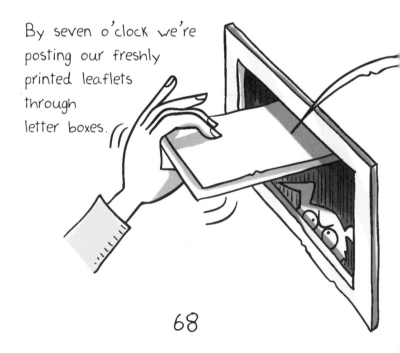

BEEHIVE ON THE ROOF OF MEADOW TOWER

My name is Melvin Meadly
(Flat 49) and I keep bees
on the roof of Meadow Tower.

Somebody has just painted a rude message on my beehive because I think they are worried about having lots of bees living near them.

PLEASE DON'T WORRY!

IMPORTANT FACT — bees can only sting once and when they do sting, their guts are pulled out and they die so they're not going to do that unless they are really upset or think they are in danger.

LEAVE THEM ALONE AND THEY WON'T HARM YOU.

EXTRA NOTE — please don't lean your bikes against my beehive, or leave litter on it, or kick footballs against it, or sit on it.

Thank you for reading my leaflet.

Melvin Meadly

and Mrs Meadly (Detective Inspector Meadly)

I lie in bed with stuff spinning around in my head.

If Crudwell is the graffiti artist, perhaps his mum and dad will see the leaflet and warn him to leave my beehive alone – to leave ME alone. That would be good, but why wouldn't the smoker work its magic? Will I ever enter the hive and be a bee again?

4

The phone wakes me. Mum is calming
somebody down:

A lump on your nose, Mrs
O'Donnell? A bee has stung
you in the night? Sorry, but
I doubt it was a bee... OK,
thank you... goodbye.

Mum puts the phone down. It rings again.

Hi, Mr Phillips... sorry?
Something's been eating
your honey? Bees? Perhaps
it's your wife or... What?
I WOULD SAY THAT,
WOULDN'T I? No, honestly
... er, well... goodbye.

'What's going on?' I ask.

Mum sighs. 'Our leaflets seem to have done more harm than good. Because most people hardly ever go up on the roof, they didn't know about your beehive until the leaflet. Now they're all freaking out and blaming everything on the bees!'

'Sorry, Mum,' I say.

'Not your fault, love,' Mum replies.

But the moaning continues for the rest of the week.

On Tuesday, old Mrs Smalling (Flat 23) calls round to complain about a swarm of bees hiding in her flat.

MY BEES HAVE SWARMED?

No – it's a false alarm. The batteries in Mrs Smalling's hearing aid are running out, which makes them buzz loudly.

Bzzzzz!
Bzzzzz!

BLASTED BEES!

On Wednesday, Mr and Mrs McKipper (Flat 11) are moaning about our bees stinging them in the night and waking up covered in itchy red bites. More like fleas, Mum and I reckon. Their manky mutt Mabel is always scratching herself.

On Thursday, we receive an odd message from Kate and Richard Sprout (Flat 33).

Hey, Melvin and Mrs Meadly!
There's a rumour going round
that you're growing peas on
the roof of Meadow Tower. We're
veggies too so if you've got any
spare peas it would be totally
cool if you wanted to trade
some for one of our mushroom
and Brussels sprout smoothies.

Take care, guys

Kate and Rich X

'BEES *NOT* PEAS – this is ridiculous, didn't they read the leaflet?' Mum groans.

On Friday, the Mothers and Toddlers group (from Meadow Hall) phone to say we shouldn't be keeping bees in the city because car fumes will pollute the honey and what happens if a child is poisoned? I want to tell them – THAT IS COMPLETE RUBBISH! But Mum explains politely that they are mistaken.

'We have got to do something.' She sighs. 'How about a meeting?'

'A meeting?' I gasp. 'But...but I'd have to talk to everybody and answer questions. They might get angry and start shouting like in assemb...'

'Assemb?' Mum says. 'What do you mean?'

'Oh...nothing,' I say and change the subject. 'Er...so where could we have a meeting? The flat is way too small.'

'Meadow Hall,' Mum says and picks up the phone to arrange a time. Once Mum gets an idea, things start to happen very quickly. Five minutes later we're sorted.

'All arranged,' she says. 'Now let's make another leaflet!'

A MEETING TO DISCUSS
MELVIN MEADLY'S BEES!
at Meadow Hall, this Thursday @ 7:00 pm
If you have any worries or questions
PLEASE COME AND CHAT! :)

Melvin Meadly and
Mrs Meadly

Mum's determined to sort this out once and for all but I'm still fretting. What will I say? Mum insists it'll be fine. She'll do most of the talking and says I'm not to worry about people being rude or causing trouble because, after all, she is a police detective inspector.

A few hours later the leaflets are printed and posted and I'm up on the roof.

I've been here every day after school, lighting the smoker and trying to enter the hive. I'm starting to think it won't happen again.

I strike a match and light the newspaper. The hive is quieter than usual today — have my bees swarmed? I need to check.

PUFF, PUFF, PUFF!

Something catches my eye. I see a face at the window in the door that leads on to the roof. It's Priti Kaur — Crudwell's sent her to spy on me!

But she vanishes as the smoke thickens and lifts me off my feet.

IT'S HAPPENING!

I hover for a moment then I'm falling, drifting downwards slowly, slowly...

FLOOMF!

I land softly.

The same sweet, smoky smell hangs in the air but this time my arrival is unnoticed.

The bees are snoozing. But why?

I search through the dozing bodies.
Where is she? Tatty wings, bent antenna... there!

'M-m-marzter?' she says sleepily. 'Izz it you?'

I shake her. 'Are you OK? Are you ill?'

'Weez going to swarm so weez eatz lotz of honey... fill up beez for long journey ... make uzz sleepy...'

THWONK!

Something hits me hard and sends me spinning across the honeycomb.

33137 snaps out of her sleep.

'Wasp, Marzter!' she cries.

WASPS – our deadly enemy:

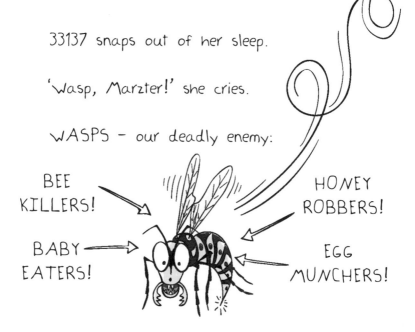

BEE KILLERS!

BABY EATERS!

HONEY ROBBERS!

EGG MUNCHERS!

Alerted, the wasp turns and grabs her.

Anger fizzes up inside me.

I charge at the attacker, catching it by surprise and knocking 33137 from its mouth.

Dazed but not damaged, she scrambles out of reach.

'Wake the workers!' I shout. 'Quick as you can!'

33137 scurries about, prodding her sisters into life. 'Wake up! Wasp attackz!'

THWACK! I'm hit again.
The stripy assassin knocks me flat.

VZZIP! It stabs me
in the arm with its
needle-sharp stinger.

The wasp's evil buzz echoes around the hive as pain sizzles through my body. Then it's on me, its ugly mug staring down as it raises its abdomen and points its stinger at my chest. Here it comes — the final, fatal sting.

My courage drains away. I feel weak and hopeless just like at school but this is more serious — I don't want to die! I squeeze my eyes shut and wait for it.

But the wasp doesn't strike. It pauses and looks up as angry buzzing fills the air.

Has help arrived? Am I going to be saved after all?

No. It is wasps not bees that appear from the darkness and they gather round to watch me meet my end.

'Zzzwah ha hahhh! Waspz lovzzz the taste of honey!' the evil bug laughs. 'And you'z stupid beez makez it for uzzz!'

But the wasp is too busy showing off to notice what's happening behind.

'GET 'EM, GIRLZZZZ!' 33137 screams and hundreds of angry bees pile into the wasps, stinging and pushing them back to the hive entrance. Too scared and weak to help, I crawl away and collapse in the shadows, watching the terrifying tangle of angry insects as they fight to the death.

The wasps bite off heads and legs with their scissor-mouths and sting again and again as they try to capture the hive. They are bigger and stronger but far fewer than the advancing army of bees.

The fight moves away as they battle towards the entrance. I crawl further into the shadows and collapse again. The poisonous sting has weakened me and I pass out.

Some time later I am shaken awake.

'Marzter! Weez won! The waspz iz gone.'

I blink and focus – even tattier wings,
and now two bent antennae...it's 33137.
My friend is alive.

But protecting the hive has been costly.
Bodies lie scattered all around amongst
the battle-scarred bees that gather in
silence on the honeycomb floor.

Queen Bee appears
from the shadows.

'ZWEEEE! You haz done well to defeat the waspz, brave girlz. I haz been watching and now I am selecting my swarmerz,' she says. 'We will build a new hive – a new world!'

SWARM ZELECTION!

NEW HIVE, NEW WORLD!

Take me, Queen!

I'z wantz to go!

Meez too!

The queen stares down.

'Zank you, Marzter, you waked uzz from our honey zleep.'

'YOU'Z SAVED UZZ!' the bees shout.

I try to smile but I feel ashamed. I warned them of the danger but my bravery didn't last long and now I am sick with sting poison and my head is spinning.

Queen Bee continues.

'WILL YOU JOIN UZZ WHEN WE SWARMZ, MARZTER?'

PLOOFFF!

I'm back on the roof.

NOOOOOO!

And Priti Kaur is still watching through the window.

Did she see me disappear? Does she know my secret? I must talk to her!

Clutching my throbbing arm, I run to the door, but when I get there she's gone. I call down the stairs and a face appears.

> There you are, love.
> Supper's ready!

5

Giant fish fingers and beans – my favourite, but I'm not enjoying them tonight. I wasn't ready to leave the hive and now I'm back here when my bees need me. I wish I'd been stronger and braver like 33137. She was bent and battered but kept battling away until the wasps were beaten.

'How's your arm? Still sore? Nasty wasp!' Mum says.

'Hmmm,' I mumble. I've got a headache and my arm is aching.

Outside there's a low rumble then a loud crack as lightning flashes and rain starts to fall.

'Oh dear!' Mum says. 'I hope people come if it's still raining tomorrow.'

But I'm not listening, my mind is on the hive.

Right now, thousands of bees are waiting to swarm and when they've gone, the new queens, fat with royal jelly, will be ready to hatch.

Then the battle will begin — a ferocious fight to decide who will be the new ruler. Will I help the new queen or leave with the swarm? Will I even get a chance to choose?

Being a boy or a bee is out of my control.

'The meeting tomorrow night,' Mum interrupts my thoughts.

94

'If it's still raining people might not want to walk across to Meadow Hall.'

Rain? RAIN! Excellent! The bees won't swarm in wet weather — I have a little more time.

'Are you listening to anything I say?' Mum says.

I'm under attack again at school. Other kids who live in Meadow Tower are chatting about tonight's meeting and spot me in the playground.

'My mum wants those bees gotten rid of – says they'll invade us and we'll wake up covered in 'em!'

'My gran's allergic to bee stings, Meadly – you'll get done for murder if they attack her!'

And, of course, Crudwell is loving it.

Looks like it's going to be, 'bye bye, bees', Bee Boy!

Even Mrs Whelks has a go at me.

You live in a busy tower block, Melvin Meadly. You can't be surprised if your neighbours are worried about bee attacks!

Bee attacks? Then I notice that Mrs Whelks is still wearing her trousers with bicycle clips.

Later, I'm up on the roof. The rain has stopped but the sky is dark and there isn't a bee in sight. But then I spot a different sort of insect. A moth. It's the one Dan told me about.

The moth lands on the hive roof and I study its markings – brown and yellow with a skull shape on its back. It is a death's head hawkmoth, another enemy of the honeybee.

This clever insect can make itself smell like a honeybee and this is how it tricks its way into the hive to drink as much honey as it can before the smell wears off and the bees recognize their enemy!

The skull stares up at me. Cupping my hands I pick the moth up and launch it off the roof. It flutters out of sight. There's no way MY hive is going to be robbed!

I leave my bees in their warm, dry home and head back down to the flat. It's time to face the neighbours.

At 6:30 p.m., Mum and I walk over to the hall in pouring rain. We put out chairs, but will anybody turn up?

Yes.

By seven o'clock the hall is packed.

Mum and I sit on stage looking down at our neighbours with their dripping umbrellas.

'Thank you for coming out in this horrible weather. Melvin and I are very sorry if our leaflet has worried you,' Mum says. 'But Melvin's bees will do you no harm.'

''Course they will! They'll sting us!' somebody shouts from the back.

'Bees should be kept in the countryside!' another neighbour says.

Dan would be angry if he heard this.

'Defend your bees!' he'd say.

Flashbacks of the rubbish assembly fill my head but they soon vanish. Since entering the hive I'm feeling stronger. Now, another battle begins but this time it's a war of words not wasps.

'Bees are important to all of us!' I say. 'Not just for honey — we need bees to keep us alive. Without bees the world can't survive! I've got a list of interesting facts that...'

But the crowd is impatient.

We don't want your boring list!

Or your honey!

I gets my honey from Mr Patel's shop!

Somebody in a hoodie walks to the front of the hall. The hood drops. It's Crudwell.

'BAN THE BEES!' he shouts.

And almost everybody joins in.

Then somebody else walks to the front
and jumps up on stage. They grab a
chair and stand on it. Then they pull an
apple from their pocket and take a bite.

It's Priti Kaur.

Apart from the sound of a girl eating an
apple there is total silence.

Priti speaks.

No bees, no pollination. No pollination,
no apples. Bees are just about the most
important insects in the whole world!

Crudwell is furious to be interrupted. Not just because it's by somebody smaller than him but because... IT'S A GIRL!

'Sit down!' he hisses.

'NO, NORMAN, I WON'T SIT DOWN!' Priti says. 'You like pizza and jam and onion rings and baked beans, don't you? Well, without bees you'll be DREAMING about food like that and living on snail soup and seaweed. Tasty, huh?'

'What do you know? You're just a kid!' Crudwell's gran shouts.

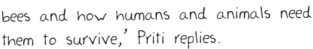

'I'm not an expert but I read about bees and how humans and animals need them to survive,' Priti replies.

Crudwell's dad jumps up wagging his finger. 'Animals? Are you nuts? Why do animals need bees?'

'Well, Mr Crudwell...' Priti takes a deep breath. 'Without bees we wouldn't have a lot of the plants and trees that make the fruit and seeds that some animals need to survive. But it's not just about food – cotton plants need bees too and without cotton we'd have no cotton T-shirts or pants either. You wear pants, don't you, Mr Crudwell?'

Mr Crudwell sits down, defeated and pink-faced but still shaking his head.

Priti looks across at me and then back to the audience.

'All I'm saying is, it's cool that Mel is keeping bees on the roof of Meadow Tower. We should be working together like bees in a hive. Please, everybody, it's very important – MEL'S HIVE MUST SURVIVE!'

There are mumbles of agreement. A man stands and starts to clap. Mr Johnson. A few more join in and soon the whole hall is clapping and cheering.

THE HIVE MUST SURVIVE!
THE HIVE MUST SURVIVE!
THE HIVE MUST SURVIVE!

I'm looking at Priti Kaur. Did she REALLY just say all that? She knows loads about bees and it seems she doesn't think I'm a joke after all. I'm confused but happy.

Mum thumps the table with her umbrella.

'Can we take a vote, neighbours? Those of you who are happy for Melvin to keep his bees, please raise your hands.'

Almost everybody.

'And those against?'

Just a few. Mostly Crudwells.

Macs are put on and umbrellas opened
as people make their way back to
Meadow Tower.

A few remain.

I feel shy but I have to
say it. 'Thanks, Priti, you
were AMAZING! I didn't
know you liked bees.'

'You never asked me,' she says.

'And thanks for your support,
Mr Johnson,' Mum adds.

At last, things are improving in my human
life but I MUST enter the hive once
more — my friends will be swarming...

I NEED TO BE A BEE AGAIN!

6

I'm on the roof and they're starting to swarm.

The air is filled with bees and I need to join them.

Puff, puff, puff.

PLEASE let it work, I pray as my shaky hands pump the smoker.

Priti wanted to watch and I'd almost told her my secret but decided to give myself a little more time.

'Too dangerous without a bee-suit,' I'd said. 'I'll ask Mum if she can alter Dan's for you.'

Puff, puff.

COME ON...

The smoke thickens and spirals. Seconds later I'm drifting down.

FLOOMF!

BUZZ F

I'm a bee again but this time I'm outside and I'm flying. Wow! It's amazing! I circle above the hive doing loop-the-loops. There's a smell in the air, a scent from the Queen Bee that the swarm will follow. I look up and there it is, a vast cloud of excited insects, morphing into different shapes and growing fast. There are thousands and thousands of bees. Finding 33137 will be impossible.

As well as bodies, buzzing voices fill the air.

So this is it. The bees are off and they want me to go with them – to leave Meadow Tower with its broken lift and Norman Crudwell and the jokes and the laughing and the teasing and miserable Mrs Whelks. I tried to tell them, to explain how incredible bees are. And now I have a chance to fly away, to join my swarm as they start their amazing adventure.

I circle around looking down at the hive – Dan's hive. Streams of bees are still leaving but the unselected will stay. I imagine Mum's voice. 'Running away is the easy choice. Dan left you in charge. Stay and sort it out, love.'

As the last few bees join the swarm I watch with wonder as they circle for a last time and swoop down to the parks and gardens below. Scout bees will fly ahead to look for the new home. Maybe a roof or a hollow tree or, if they're lucky, an empty hive.

And then it comes to me. I've been caught up in the swirling swarm of excitement but I can't leave. I don't want to. I'll stick with my old world. I'll stay with my hive and help the new queen.

The noisy excitement of the swarm is replaced with gentle buzzing as I fly down to the hive. I land and guard bees check me over with gentle prods like security at an airport.

Inside it is quieter than usual. More than half the bees have left. Until the new queen has mated with the drones there will be no new bees.

I watch as workers calmly go about their business — the circle of life continues.

A tatty old bee approaches.

Marzter, you'z stayed!

It's 33137, my favourite bee.

'You too,' I say.

'Yezz, not selected — too old,' 33137
replies. 'Come, we needz to check the
queenz.'

I follow my friend along the honeycomb
path to where big queen cells have been
made. The specially chosen larvae have
finished their feast of royal jelly. Inside
their cells they are growing fast and
changing into queens.

One of the cells is bulging — it's opening!

'Look, Marzter, first queen hatching!'

Other workers join us. 'QUEENZ COMING!' they shout.

The wax cap lifts like a submarine hatch and a queen emerges.

'ZWEEEEEEEEEEE!' she cries, announcing her arrival.

But she doesn't wait for another queen to hatch and challenge her. There are easier ways to win the war. Crawling from her cell, she moves to another that has not yet opened.

'ZWEEEEEEEEEEE!'

Nature has cruel ways of selecting leaders.

'Look, Marzter, she sting through cell, kill other queen before she hatch!' 33137 says.

Her victim doesn't stand a chance. But there are twelve queen cells and while the first queen scurries around killing her unborn rivals, others are hatching and preparing to fight.

'Needz to be quick, Marzter!'

But she is not quick enough.

Three new queens have escaped their cells and are ready to clash with the first-born.

Tumbling over the honeycomb they must fight or die.

33137 is excited. 'Zey stab with their stingerz! Queen beez can stingz lotz of timezz!'

'STING, STING, STING!' the bees cry.

Two queens roll away and curl up. Pumped with poison, they will soon be dead.

The remaining queens are exhausted but with a last effort, the first queen grabs her rival in a deadly grip and plunges her stinger into its body. It is a killer blow.

She moves away to rest but eager nurse bees are already tending to their new queen.

Suddenly...

What's happening?
Has another queen hatched?

And then I see them — two huge black eyes staring down at us.

'Death's head hawkmoth!' I shout, but 33137 and the other workers are confused. The moth approaches slowly. Sharp blades glisten on its feet. One swipe would slice half a dozen bees in half.

'Look, there!' I say. 'In front of you!' But the workers are blind. And then I remember. The moth's scent is tricking them!

I'm face to face with it.

'Terribly forry!' the death's head hawkmoth says in a strange, royal sort of voice. 'But I don't fink they can see me!' And then it laughs. 'Hoff, hoff, hoff! It's my scent you thee, I thmell like a bee and can sound rarffer like a bee too! ZWEEEEE what I mean?'

'Get lost or we'll sting you to death!' I shout.

'Hoff, hoff! I don't fink so,' the moth sniggers. 'I'fe been waiting for the queen to hatch so I can f-f-finish her offf! No queen, no hife! All the honey will be mine!'

Kill the queen? No way. I jump on the moth but my stinger is useless on its armoured skin. It shrugs me off and slashes at me with its blades. I dodge as they gash into the honeycomb floor.

'Fuper duper yummy honey!' it cries as the sticky stuff spills out. 'Clear off, bee, I'fe got a woyal engagement!'

Pushing me aside it looks around for the queen. But the death's head hawkmoth has been hiding in the hive for a long time and its bee scent has finally worn off.

At last, 33137 and the other workers can smell the danger and charge at the enormous insect.

'KILL DEATH MOTH!' they cry, smashing into their enemy.

But the moth brushes them aside like an elephant mildly bothered by ants.

'ZWEEEEEE!' It's a glass-shattering scream. 'OUT HOFF MY WAY!'

33137 and her friends land in a heap of wings and legs.

But 33137 hasn't given up. Her voice is weak. 'Marzter!' she whispers, pointing to a honeycomb cell. 'Eat, getz strong!'

Royal jelly! I stick my head in and gulp some down. The effect is instant. Energy ripples through my body.

I am a warrior!

But the moth has found the queen. Still exhausted, she is unable to fight back as it crushes her with its powerful legs.
I fly onto the moth's head, grabbing its antennae and snapping them off.

ZWEEE!

The scream is even louder this time and I'm sent flying by its fluttering wings. I lie dazed, vaguely aware that I'm about to be slashed. The death's head hawkmoth opens its mouth for one last ear-piercing scream.

Thinking fast, I grab a lump of honeycomb and, just as the moth starts to scream, I ram the beeswax into its mouth.

The moth's eyes bulge with horror. Unable to stop, the scream inflates the bunged-up bug into a furry balloon. It grows bigger and bigger...

HMMM

The moth explodes in a soggy shower of
legs and wings. Another battle won.

The new queen is a little crumpled but
not seriously hurt. She has only just
hatched but seems to know who I am
and what I've done.

'Youz save uzz again, Marzter. Zank you.'

Death moth dead!

New queenz zafe!

But 33137 doesn't join in. I help the tired old bee back onto her feet.

'The royal jelly was a great idea!' I say, trying to cheer her up. But it's a while before 33137 replies.

'I'z hurt, Marzter,' she whispers. 'But I'z got something important to...to...tell youz...

33137's voice is fading. I lean close.

'Marzter, we'z needz you...'

Huh? Need me? NEED ME TO
WHAT? What was 33137 trying to tell
me?

I grab the smoker and pump.

140

For the next few days I try over and over, but it is impossible to enter the hive again.

I should be happy –

🐝 Our neighbours say it's OK for me to have my hive on the roof.

🐝 My bees have swarmed successfully.

🐝 I have a new queen.

🐝 We have won our battles against the wasps and the moth.

🐝 It will soon be time to collect honey.

🐝 And, of course, I have my new friend, Priti.

We're walking to school. The rain clouds have disappeared and the sun is shining. We haven't stopped chatting since Priti's amazing speech in Meadow Hall. It's like we've always been friends.

'I like you because you're quiet,' Priti says. 'Not always showing off, like the others. And you keep bees – how cool is that?'

'Er, quite cool?' I say.

'VERY cool, Bee Boy!' Priti replies.

'I thought you were always laughing at me,' I admit, my face turning pink, and we discuss my rubbish talk at assembly and Norman Crudwell's buzzing and Mrs Whelks's pants.

'It was hilarious!' Priti says. 'And anyway, I laugh at everything. Dad says seeing the funny side of things is the best way to be.'

And Priti's right. When I think about it now, the rubbish assembly was quite funny.

And then I ask Priti why she was spying on me through the window.

'I'm interested in bees,' she says. 'So I watched to see how you were getting on. I should have asked, sorry!'

I want to be clear about everything. 'And why did you call me a loser?' I ask.

'Eh? When?' Priti says.

'On the stairs, just past Crudwell's flat on your way home.'

'OH, THAT!' Priti laughs. 'Crudwell had been teasing me – asking if I was going to see my boyfriend. Meaning you!'

'And?' I say.

'And I was on my phone, you idiot! I was telling Mum that Crudwell was hanging around outside his flat and being horrible again. I was telling her that he is SUCH A LOSER!'

'Oh,' I say. How could I have got it all so wrong?

But then, as usual, my thoughts turn to bees. I drift off into thought. I didn't get a chance to say goodbye to 33137, and what was she trying to tell me? Is she still alive? If I could enter the hive just once more I might be able to find out.

'What are you thinking about?' Priti asks.

'Huh? Oh, bees, I guess.'

'Stupid question!' she laughs. 'Has your mum managed to alter Dan's suit yet?'

Mum finished it a few days ago; I can't delay any longer. The bees had told me not to tell anyone but I can't keep Priti away from the hive forever. Would it matter if she did discover my secret? It might even be good to share it.

'Yeah, it's done,' I say. 'Come and try it on tonight and we'll check the bees together.'

COOL!

There's another reason I should be happy. Today is Mrs Whelks's last day. Last morning, actually – Miss Springfield, our new teacher, starts this afternoon.

Some of us have brought presents in. We put them on Mrs Whelks's desk as we come into class: a chocolate pig, lavender deodorant, a candle in the shape of a skull, a bunch of flowers (picked from somebody's garden by Crudwell), a book about donkeys, and from me (well, Mum really) a jar of beeswax face cream. I told Mum how much Mrs Whelks likes bees.

'Thank you, Melvin,' Mrs Whelks says, peering suspiciously at the jar. 'No need to look so glum, I'm sure the new teacher will be just as nice as me.'

The morning passes and it's soon time to wave goodbye to Mrs Whelks as she removes the bicycle clips and gets in her car.

And it's true – Miss Springfield is nice; in fact, MUCH nicer than Mrs Whelks. We hear about her dogs and how she lives in the countryside and keeps chickens and grows fruit and vegetables.

Perhaps I'll enjoy school a bit more now.

I'm following Priti up on to the roof. Mum has done a great job on Dan's bee-keeper's suit. But I don't feel good. The bees told me not to share our secret. Am I letting them down? I know Mr Johnson didn't see anything, but he's a grown-up – it might be different with Priti.

'Put a bit of crumpled newspaper in the smoker, please. Wait for the flames – now grab a handful of wood shavings...'

I'm shaking.

'Are you OK?' Priti asks.

'Er, yeah, I'm fine. Add some shavings ...that's it,' I say.

The shavings catch and I close the smoker. This is it, I can't keep it to myself any longer... I really want Priti to enter the hive with me.

A cloud of smoke covers us and when it clears...

Priti is still standing there and so am I.

'Cough! Do you really need that much smoke, Mel?' Priti splutters.

'Er, no, not really,' I admit, and suddenly feel pleased that nothing happened. The moment has passed. I'd risked sharing my secret but feel relief that it is still safe. Perhaps the bees saved me.

We open the hive and check the frames. I explain that there are fewer bees because they recently swarmed. The new queen needs to make her maiden flight before she can lay eggs to make more bees.

'Maiden flight?' Priti asks.

'The young queen will leave the hive and mate with the male bees...'

'Drones?' Priti interrupts.

'Yeah. The drones follow her, mate in the air then drop from the sky – DEAD!'

Priti scrunches her face. 'Ooh!'

The frames are heavy with honey.

'How d'you get it out?' Priti asks.

'With a honey extractor. You put the frames in it and spin them around.'

'Where are you going to get one of those?'
Priti says.

It's a good question but I have a plan.

I persuade Mum to drive me over to
Daisy's house. I could have walked but
I'm hoping we'll have something heavy
to bring home with us. Daisy is pleased
to see me and very happy that my bees
have made lots of honey.

'Take care, bring it back clean,'
she says. 'And you are
welcome to borrow
my extractor.'

'Thanks, Daisy,' I say. 'How's Dan? He said he'd email me.'

'I think he's OK, Mel,' Daisy says. 'But there's often no Internet in the places he's working. I haven't heard from him for ages either. Bees are in trouble all around the world and Dan's trying to help. I know he's busy but I'm sure he'll be in touch soon.'

And then it's time to go. 'Thank you very much, Mrs King,' Mum says. 'I have a colleague who patrols this area, he'll bring the extractor back next week.'

We drive home in silence. I'm pleased about the extractor and hoping Daisy will remind Dan to send me an email.

Back at Meadow Tower, Mr Johnson carries the extractor up to the roof for us and after removing the frames, Priti helps me spin the honey out.

By the time we've finished we have
twenty-eight full jars on the kitchen table.

Mum suggests we should give some to the
neighbours who supported us.

We work our way up delivering jars from
the ground floor to the top, and then we
check on the bees. It was raining earlier
but the sun is out now and should have
dried and warmed the hive.

Maybe today... if I
could just make it happen
one more time...

Mr Johnson is standing
by the hive shaking his
head. Something is wrong.

'Bad news, Mel,' he says.
But he doesn't need to
say any more.

Somebody has taken the roof off the hive. I peer down into the soggy mess. Bees need to be warm and dry but the rain has soaked and chilled their home.

IT'S OVER. 33137, THE NEW QUEEN AND ALL THE OTHER BEES ARE DEAD. I WILL NEVER BE A BEE AGAIN!

'Oh, Mel!' Priti sobs, clutching my arm. 'Your poor bees. Who did this?'

It's a hot day and the classroom windows are open.

'Today we're going to find out about plants!' Miss Springfield says. 'I need a volunteer to be a tree. Somebody big and strong!'

Norman Crudwell is keen to show Miss Springfield that he is the strongest person in the class.

'I'll do it, Miss!' he says.

What Crudwell doesn't realize is that he will have to wear the tree outfit that Miss Springfield has brought in.

'I made it myself!' she says. 'It'll fit you a treat, Norman.'

Crudwell is not happy about the outfit but he volunteered and it's too late to back out. So there he is standing at the front of the class with his arms outstretched looking like... well, a tree.

On his feet he's wearing wellies that have been painted to look like roots.

'The roots suck up water and minerals that the tree needs to grow...' Miss Springfield says.

Crudwell's arms are sprouting branches and he's wearing a big hat to make the tree taller.

Miss Springfield continues, 'Sunlight is very important for plants. The leaves on a tree...'

Something's happening.

I'm daydreaming about queen bees, dead bees and my bee friend 33137 when I hear buzzing outside.

BZZZZZZ!

'...sprout buds in the spring, which soon...'

The buzzing is getting louder.

Wow! It's a swarm of bees. They're looking for somewhere to rest and it looks like they've spotted the ideal place.

'...open out into leaves...' Miss Springfield stops.

The swarm flies in through the open window and lands on the hat of 'Crudwell the Tree'.

There are shrieks of horror from the class as Norman Crudwell stands frozen in terror with the insect invaders clinging to his hat.

'Oh, my goodness! Now don't panic, Norman,' Miss Springfield says in a panicky voice. She tries to open the classroom door but Crudwell is blocking the way and each time Miss Springfield reaches for the door handle the swarm buzzes angrily.

'Help!' Crudwell cries quietly, terrified that if he shouts it will make the bees even angrier. 'They're on my face!'

'Oh dear, we need a bee person!' Miss Springfield says.

'Mel keeps bees, Miss!' Priti calls out.

Crudwell is sobbing.

'Melvin?' asks Miss Springfield.

My classmates stop staring at the sobbing tree and look across to me.

A bee expert is urgently needed and, I guess, that's me! I'VE ACTUALLY BEEN A BEE! To be honest, I'm more interested in helping the bees than Norman Crudwell but I don't have to tell him that.

'Don't worry, Norman,' I say. 'The bees sound angry but they're not really. Swarming bees don't often sting because before they leave the hive they eat lots of honey and being so full makes them calm...'

'NEVER MIND THE BEE LESSON – GET THEM OFF ME!' Crudwell screams and the swarm replies with an even louder

BZZZZZZZZ!

Then Crudwell admits it.

I'm sorry for what I did, right? I won't do nothing again... JUST HELP ME!

He's blubbing loudly now.

So it WAS Crudwell who killed my bees. Priti and I had guessed as much. But this swarm is very much alive and I'm going to save them.

'Shhhh!' I say. 'Don't be a baby, Norman! Keep still.'

167

'Can I help?' Priti asks.

'I need to shake the swarm into a box or basket,' I say.

'The waste-paper bin?' Priti suggests, grabbing the big plastic bin that sits by Miss Springfield's desk.

'Brilliant! Norman, you need to...'

Miss Springfield interrupts. 'Are you sure you know what you're doing, Melvin?'

'Yes, Miss. We need to get the bees in the bin!' I say.

The class gasps.

'REALLY?' Miss Springfield asks anxiously.

I take the bin from Priti and hold it under the terrified tree.

'Now shake your head and they'll drop off!' I tell Crudwell.

The trembling tree does as it's told. There's a loud buzz… then… nothing.

'Again!' I say.

Once more Crudwell shakes and this time the swarm, or most of it, drops off.

I give the buzzing bin to Priti.

'I'm going outside, Priti. Pass me the bin through the window,' I say. 'Now, move away from the door, Norman.'

I run outside and down the side of the school to our classroom windows.

'There are still lots of bees buzzing around in here!' Miss Springfield calls out.

'Don't worry, Miss!' I shout. 'As long as the queen bee is in the bin the others will follow her scent.'

Priti passes the bin to me and as I move away from the window the other bees follow.

'Wait for me!' Priti says, climbing out after me. 'We can put them in your empty hive!'

'But I haven't dried it out and cleaned it,' I say.

Priti is smiling. 'Mr Johnson and I have done it for you. It was going to be a surprise.'

'That's amazing! Thank you! Tell Miss Springfield what we're doing and I'll see you up on the roof!'

Half an hour later, we have carried the bin full of bees on to the roof of Meadow Tower and tipped it into my clean, dry beehive. Priti and Mr Johnson have even painted over the graffiti.

We leave the bees to sort out their new home and return to school. When we enter the classroom, everybody claps.

Even Miss Springfield joins in.

'Thank you, Priti, for bravely assisting
Melvin. And well done to you, Melvin!
I think there's somebody who owes you
both an extra special thank you. And he
didn't even get stung – well, just a few
times, on the end of his nose.'

No longer dressed
as a tree, Crudwell
stands. His nose is
very red.

'Danks,' he mutters,
in a swollen, bunged-up
sort of voice.

Miss Springwell continues, 'It was
marvellous the way you took control of
the situation, Melvin – simply marvellous!'

The class cheers even louder than they
did in the rubbish assembly. But this time
it makes me smile.

Epilogue

Dan sent an email. He's been helping bee-keepers in countries where bees are in trouble. He says scientists aren't sure why beehives around the world are dying but it's a big, BIG problem. They think it could be caused by the sprays that farmers use on their crops. Or maybe it's mites and viruses infecting hives or wild-flower meadows disappearing or even pollution from cars and factories. Dan's been busy trying to find out. He says it's great that our hive is doing well. He told me to keep in touch and that he hopes to see us when he gets back.

I haven't seen Mum smile so much in ages.

Every day, after school, I check my hive. The roof is tidier now — no cola cans or crisp packets.

Sometimes I light my smoker and check inside but I haven't become Bee Boy since my first swarm died.

If I did, perhaps I could find out what 33137 was trying to tell me. All I can do is keep puffing my smoker and hoping it will happen again.

⬡⬡⬡⬡⬡⬡⬡

Priti is with me on the roof when we hear a strange buzzing noise in the hive.

'Doesn't sound normal,' she says.

I'm glad I didn't tell Priti my secret. The bees told me not to and I nearly let them down. It would have blown everything.

I press my ear to the roof of the hive. It's like I've put earphones on — the buzzing is much louder. Except it's not just buzzing — I can hear words! The bees are whispering to me...

'Hear anything?' Priti asks.

I hold up my hand to hush her and concentrate on the whispering.

TROUBLEZ AHEADZZ...
PROTECT UZZZ, MARZTER!

Priti is studying my face. 'Well?'

'They're just excited,' I lie.

I look away, frowning to hide my excitement.

MY NEW SWARM IS TALKING TO ME!

Then I smile. 'Let's leave them alone and check them tomorrow when they've calmed down,' I say. But my mind is buzzing. What kind of trouble? Is this what 33137 was trying to tell me?

Does this mean I'll get to be Bee Boy again?

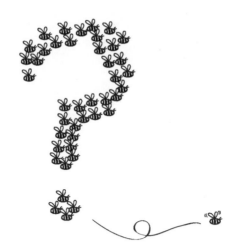

Melvin's list of interesting bee facts that he didn't get a chance to read out in Meadow Hall (see page 102)

1

A worker bee only lives for 6 weeks.

2

One bee will make one twelfth of a teaspoon of honey in its lifetime.

3

Bees will fly 50,000 miles and visit two million flowers to make one jar of honey.

4 A bee can carry its own weight in pollen and nectar.

5 A queen bee can lay a quarter of a million eggs in a year.

6 The language of the waggle dance was decoded by Karl von Frisch 50 years ago.

7 At the end of the summer, drones that haven't mated with a new queen are thrown out from the hive to die.

GET OUT!

About the Author

Tony De Saulles worked as a book designer before turning to illustration and writing. He lives in the countryside and is learning to be a bee-keeper.

Tony has been illustrating Scholastic's best-selling Horrible Science series for 20 years and sold more than ten million copies in over thirty countries.

Bee Boy is his first project with Oxford University Press.

www.tonydesaulles.co.uk

Acknowledgements

Special thanks to my literary agent, Sarah Such, for helping bring Bee Boy to life, to Jon Appleton for his help and encouragement and finally to Liz, Gill, and Lizzie at OUP for their enthusiasm and belief in the book.

Look out for book 2!

BEE BOY

Attack of the Zombees

Tony De Saulles

'A bee-rilliant read from bee-ginning to end' —NICK SHARRATT

Here are some other books
that we think you'll love!